A Reflection of Life

BOOK OF
POEMS AND
SHORT STORIES

Pamela Douglas

Sometimes in life things happen to you that you would never believe would happen; because you think it happens to other people; not you.

"I did not see it, but you said it was there all along. You said I just needed to give birth to the creativity in me. Your words were like a looking glass held up in front of me so I could see.   To see what I took as nothing, you showed me it was something."

"Thank you to my beautiful sister Patricia, thank you for always encouraging me, you are the best."

Thank you to Kyle, Marilyn and Michael for your support and encouragement

ISBN 978-1-9160942-5-3

Publisher: Here 4 You Publishing (UK) Ltd

Typeset by TamaRe House Publishers Ltd, UK

Author: Pamela Douglas

Contents

"I skip along the clouds and dance with the wind and got lost in the thrill of it."

I AM JEALOUS

The wind breezes through her hair and cools her warm face as it passes. Her face is raised up to the sky, arms stretched out. How beautiful the wind is as it blows gently on her face. Eyes closed, she imagined flying in the air like a bird. Her arm raises up to dance a waltz with the wind. She did not need music.

She stood there in the middle of the path, the wind blowing lightly around her as it moved softly and brushes her face, she felt happy at that moment. The breeze gave her a sense of freedom, surrounded by trees she opened her eyes slowly.   It was only her imagination.

The wind is blowing and lightly touches the branches, the leaves drop in slow motion and cover the ground like a blanket in a circle around the tree with gold, brown, yellow and green. It is an artist's dream to capture such beauty.

Looking around me mesmerised whispering to herself she said,

"I am jealous of trees because their branches get to dance with the wind. It moves gently through the leaves. The movement causes the branches to wave. It brushes subtly against my face as it breezes by, gliding around the branches. The dance is gentle and soft, smooth, and swift like a ballerina pirouetting around and around and only stands still when the music stops. Just like the branches stop moving when the winds cease to dance!"

"I am jealous!"

"I am jealous of the rain as it dances a salsa-like movement with the wind, in a playful way."

"I am jealous of the waves as the wind creeps silently along and dances with the water. The dance is at first gentle, then strong like a crescendo against the rocks that make the waves flip flop and rise so high, it is the highlight of the surfer. This entices the surfer to ride along the shifting waves on their board."

"The waves then come crashing down suddenly splash, into a ripple along the sandy and pebbly beach. The strong winds flip flop along the water like a trapeze act in a circus and stop for a moment. Then the dance with the waves begins again slowly."

The wind is moving angrily knocking over and destroying everything that lies in its path. It's twisting and spinning around fast like a whirlwind, it is a tornado and not in a mood to dance but let itself be heard with a loud gutsy tempestuous noise, it's furious.

"I am not jealous of the trees or waves when it performs like this."

Here comes the sun as it pushes slowly through and tells the wind to calm down. The wind gently touches my face with its warm breeze, moves around the trees and dances with the branches. The wind quicksteps along the leaves and causes the branches to sway from side to side in a dance, like someone trying to find the movement of a dance for the first time.

"I am jealous!"

My Name is Love

Love looks out for you, dressed up for you.

Love is scared to come near, comes so far like the tide, and turns back.

Love wants to see you but is afraid.

Love reaches out to you.

Love don't want you to go.

Love waits patiently.

Love misses you.

Love refuses to leave.

Love sheds a tear.

Love hides to protect itself from you.

Love is put into a time vault and released at the appropriate moment.

Love runs away and takes a sabbatical.

Love plays hide and seek with you.

Love resides in the maisonette of the chest and shares it with affection.

My name is Love

CHANGE THE PICTURE

The weather changes from sunshine to rain, rain to sunshine. It is easy to change trains, change addresses and change your mind but to change the picture of your way of life, you look for reasons why you cannot do it.

The picture is hanging on the wall you have had it for a while now. If you are honest, it has been there since you were a child, you grew up with it. What is it about this picture that you do not want to get rid of it, the picture makes you feel safe, you have got used to it and what would you replace it with? You want to replace it, but you cannot, you think you are stuck with it because you have had it for so long.

You are asked with curiosity. "Why do you have that picture?"

Puzzled at what you were being asked, you say.

"I do not know what to change it with." Sounding hopeless.

Sometimes you do not even notice it, others can see it, but you cannot see that the picture did not look right where it was and there was something wrong with the picture.

Your life is like that picture, yet you could not see that your life needed to be changed but if you did see, how would you change it; where would you start; or what would you do about it; In your mind it seen as if your life is spinning around till you feel dizzy that you fall, and you just stay there because it is difficult for you to get up.   Time had stood still, and everything seen to be moving fast and quickly around you, like sitting on the Waltzer at a funfair and being push faster and faster as it goes around and around. The negative words are like the Waltzer and becomes instrumental in you not doing anything to change the picture of your life. You are stuck there unable to move from the words of,

 "You will never be any good at that!"

 "You will never be able to do it!"

The never, had you stuck because you believe the words that was said to you. You got so used to the negative words spoken to you, that when someone said something positive to you, you do not believe them. Why would you believe them?

"They were just saying what they think you want to hear" were your thoughts.

Because being told negative words like:

"You are stupid!"

"You are an idiot!"

"You are a fool!"

"You are rubbish!"

"You are useless!"

"You are no good!"

That you believed they were your middle names given to you at birth, since that is all you heard, why would you believe any different. Sometimes even your behaviour was affected by the negative names you were called as the time machine of the past take you back when you hear. "You are such a fool; why would you do that." Which causes you to react.

"How do you change the negative picture of your life?" when it had left you with feelings of anxiety, lack of confidence always wanting reassurance and looking for acceptance from others, making poor choices and wrong decisions. You think that you are not deserving of anything good and find it hard to accept gifts given to you because you are suspicious of everyone and everything, especially when someone give you a compliment. If you are shown kindness or someone is nice to you, you say to yourself.

"What are they after, they must want something?"

And a thousand questions of why; flood your thoughts, still; you are wanting to fit in to be a part of something and you were not fussy as long as they listen to what you had to say, though you know that you would get nervous and stay quiet. Words would have a hard time coming out of your mouth in case you said something that would cause them to say.

"That is a stupid thing to say." or "Don't be so stupid."

You secretly wanted to be a person that was clever and interesting to be with, but you did not realise that you were already clever and smart because you allowed yourself to be believe all the negative words you were told. You had a lot to offer, yet they could not see that.

You were always staring out the window, as if you are on the lookout for those alien ships in the sky, they keep talking about on the discovery channel. You complain that you are bored, and you want to do something different, something exciting, something challenging but you still stand there at the same place stuck not moving.

Instruction manual of what to do came from different sources, marked.

"You can do this!"

"You can change it!"

"This is what you do!"

"This is how you do it!"

Barriers like ear plugs shutting out the many voices of opinions and advice given to you.

However, it all has no meaning to you, so you ignore them with their instructions. Maybe you are too comfortable or maybe you are afraid of the change. You want to do it yourself but do not know how; you feel helpless because negative words have been the building blocks which formed a foundation for your existence.

One-day sitting on one of the benches in the park, you noticed a leaflet on the ground and pick it up because it looked interesting and read the words on the leaflet which said.

"Change the picture of your way of life!"

And as you sat there reading you started laughing. This was like a release for you, you understood now, the penny had finally dropped and you were able to see clearly for the first time, what you needed to do in order to change the picture of your way of life.

WHAT IS FEAR?

Sometimes our reaction to fear is like metal to a magnet stuck in one place unable to move. Fear can sometimes take control of our life.

Fear of the unknown.

Fear of what you believe or think might happen.

Fear to open the door.

Fear of losing control.

Fear of dying.

Fear to step outside.

Fear of heights.

Fear of noises.

Fear of crowds.

Fear to speak.

Fear to answer the phone.

Fear to be alone.

Fear to let go.

Fear to look at you.

Fear to love and be loved.

Fear of messing up.

Fear of what?

What is fear to you?

"DON'T LET FEAR TAKE CONTROL OF YOUR LIFE!"

I AM SORRY

Sorry is a word, we find hard to say but it is never too late to say it.

I am sorry I was not there for you before.

I am sorry I did not take much notice of you.

I am sorry I did not keep my promise to you.

I am sorry I was caught up in my own emotions.

I am sorry I did not listen to you.

I am sorry I did not mean it that way.

I am sorry I did not look for you.

I am sorry I did not tell you how much I love you.

I am sorry I did not know that it upset you.

I am sorry for what I said to you.

I am sorry I did not take you with me.

I am sorry for how I left you.

I am sorry for what you had to go through.

I am so sorry.

ONE

SOMETIMES IN LIFE YOU ARE TOLD THIS:

One thing you must know, you only have one life.

One thing you could do.

One thing you should not do.

One thing you can change.

One thing can change your life.

One thing you can leave behind.

One way in or one way out.

One meaning.

One word said.

One person to believe in you.

One last chance.

One last time.

One thing I told you to do.

One thing that is missing.

One place you do not go.

One thing you must see.

One thing that remain.

One thing I must show to you.

One thing!

SADNESS

Lost in your emotions, it is like a ship lost at sea and cannot see its way back to land.

When you are lost in your emotions, you only see your pain, your hurt and your suffering, that is all you see.   You do not see anyone else's pain, distress, sadness, and misery or the struggles of others not even the unhappiness of your children.   You focus only on yourself; you think that you are the only one going through the things that happen to you and no one knows, how you feel when you get lost in your emotions and sadness.

Sadness, you are there hovering I am afraid to let you in, you might stay longer than I want you to stay, darkness quietly and slowly wants to creep in behind me and cover me like a blanket, stopping me from seeing my way out and be rescued by happiness from the grip of your control. That is why I am not entertaining you.

"Don't let sadness take the place of happiness and peace of mind."

I NEVER KNEW

Sometimes we make assumptions when we do not know, we assume too much and then we find out how it is, what really happened.

I never knew why you left home, I never knew

I never knew it was my fault why you left the job

I never knew you came looking for me after I had gone

I never knew how much you loved me

I never knew I was the reason you came

I never knew you did not know, I never knew

I never knew it was not you

I never knew that is what you meant, I never knew

I never knew I was an inspiration to you

I never knew you were hurting for so long

I never knew you were listening, I never knew

I never knew that you saw me

I never knew you would help me

I never knew you were there, I never knew

I never knew what happened to you, I never knew

I never knew what you were going through

I never knew you did not want to go, I never knew

I never knew you were in so much pain

I never knew

UNEXPECTED

You are walking with confidence and you are looking good, you know it and so do others. The glances and the head turnings are confirmation. Everything is going well for you. You have so many friends that the address book is not big enough and you have to put them in a file on your computer, under names and address.

Everyone wants to be introduced to you, the phone ringing constantly; you really need a receptionist or a PA. You got invited to all their parties and events, they want you there. You must go because you add flavour, like salt and pepper with a touch of chilli sauce to their events and parties.

Then without warning one day. Bang! the thunder bolt of life conditions hits you, unexpectedly.

Behind it, Bang! Hail stones of life situations, start raining down heavy, knocking you off your feet.

Before you had time to get up again, Bang! Here comes thunder and lightning of life circumstances.

Because all this had suddenly hit you, you wanted to run and hide away.

You did not see it coming like a boxer's right hook, BANG! and you were on the floor.

You went on lock down, locked in and your sleep went for a long walk and struggled to find its way back, as if you were on a waking night shift.

You watch the hand of the clock change from hour to hour and the only sound you heard was tick tock, tick tock, tick tock and you were tempted to throw the clock in the dust bin but instead you put it in a another room because it was your grandmother's, which held a sentimental value and it was also the only clock you had.

Your confidence took a dive and got lost in the deep ocean of depression and found difficulty in reaching the surface of calmness.

After much struggle, you eventually resurfaced and found it difficult to trust anyone.

You found you were crying all the time in despair and you wanted to tell yourself to.

 "Stop it and pull yourself together."

You could not, this was not like you, you did not cry so easily before but the unexpected of the unexpected happened, suddenly.

And now you are like this.

You took a long walk down memory lane, hoping to find some comfort and laugh about it to yourself, to give a little ease to how you were feeling, that did not work.

The only friend you now have, is you and your circle of friends are the imaginary ones on the TV soap dramas. You used to say that anyone watching the soap dramas on TV did not have a life. Now you have joined the 'do not have a life' group.

Your phone had not rung for such a long time, so you kept checking to see if it was working, you remembered when your phone used to be always busy.

So, you decided to close the address file on your computer, you no longer needed it, it is family only in your address book now.

You sat there with your face resting on your hands, eyes closed, looking back at your life wondering.

You now would fit into the.

"Once Upon a Time."   story book.

"Once upon a time you had it all!"

"Once upon a time it was only the best for you!"

"Once upon a time you got whatever you wanted!"

"Once upon a time you didn't ask how much things cost or look at the price tag you bought it!"

"Once upon a time the shop assistant knew your name and what you liked!"

"Once upon a time you were with the elite of the elite!"

"Once upon a time you belonged to an exclusive club affiliated with your peers!"

"Once upon a time people were interested in what you had to say!"

Shaking your head with disappointment, you kept saying,

"Once upon a time. Once upon a time. Once upon a time!"

You could have been the main character in the invisible man story because now you are invisible to those you once associated with and went everywhere together.

You used to say living on the dole was being lazy and now you are sitting at the same place waiting for your name to be called looking around nervously, hoping no one you knew saw you. It seems as if it was taking a long time for your name to be called, that when a seat became vacant, you almost ran and sat down without hearing your name called.

"You do not belong here; you should have worn a disguise," were your thoughts as you covered your face because of embarrassment.

You had said you would never work for less than, now you are being offered less than, the less than the amount, and you would have to take it.

Desperation could have you feeling as if you were in a wrestler's hold and there is no way of getting free.

You did not know what to do, where to go, who to talk to, you were unhappy, and you felt lonely as if you were on an island all by yourself.

You had made attempts to call certain people that you knew but you felt embarrassed and what would you say to them. You were not part of their circle of friends anymore. When they had their gathering, your invite must have been lost in the do not associate anymore bin.

You had to move back home and live with your mother; dad sadly had died. Then one day you were waiting at the bus stop when the unexpected happened. You saw someone from your past that you knew, a long, long time ago at the beginning of the chapter of your life when your life was nonsensical in your eyes and not interesting.

You went to the same school and after school you would go swimming and spent the holidays together; in fact, she was your best friend.

Then both your lives took different routes and direction along life road. Doors were opened to you with various opportunities that saw your life change for the better, you moved away and moved on with your life, leaving them behind.

You are ashamed to say but you remember hurrying along quickly when you were with your new friends, not wanting them to see who you once associated with. Anytime you would bump into the best friend, you always pretended you hardly knew, who they were. Even sometimes walking into the nearest shop to hide, you desperately tried to avoid them.

When you had no choice, it was a quick hello and a goodbye wave. You behave as if you were from a privileged background and they were of a lower class, that you do not associate with.

Smiling with you, they would say with a hug,

"We must meet up; it's been a long time."

They were happy to see you!

Putting on your fake smile, your reply would be.

"That would be nice, but I am very busy at the moment, I would have to check my diary." Exaggerating busy.

Or

"I'll give you a call."

Knowing you had deleted their number a long time ago.

And after they were gone, it is out of sight and out of mind and put away in your forgotten file under,

"Who were they again?"

"I do not remember them!"

"Not interested!"

Waiting at the bus stop, you tried looking the other way so took out your newspaper staring at it as not to make eye contact. Then sadly, you heard your name called.

"Oh hello." you said. "How are you?"

Hoping your bus would come anytime soon.

Then they said with excitement in their voice.

"I am glad that I ran into you because I saw you sitting in the job centre when I stopped off to give my companies information, to advertise our job vacancies. We have vacancies in one of our branches for an administrator assistant, would you be interested?"

You gave them a blank stare. Embarrassed and feeling guilty of how you once felt towards them. You remembered your treatment to them before, that you could not answer straight away. You wanted to say no, no, no thank you, you were ok you did not need their help, but,

"Yes, yes, yes thank you," fell out of your mouth.

They told you a little about their life, they said they had been helping at the local community centre doing some volunteering work. It started after they left school and continued through to now, they were not able to do as much as before but when it is convenient, they help where they can. They also told you that they were the CEO.

Your mouth dropped open with shock and you tried to hide it by coughing, this was a big surprise when you heard what they said. In your mind you kept saying.

"CEO, CEO wow, how was this possible, when did this happen and how?"

"It is a good thing that they can't read your mind," you thought.

They wrote down the information that you needed for the job and how much the pay would be.

"It is not much but I don't care because it is better than nothing," you whispered to yourself with relief.

You were thankful because this was so incredible and what you would call, "Unexpected."

IT'S OK TO CRY, TO CRY IT'S OK

You are crying and no one can see your tears.

You are screaming and no one can hear you.

You are hurting and no one can see your pain.

You are standing there, and they cannot see you.

You are speaking and they are not listening, they want someone to listen to them.

It is ok to cry, to cry it's ok.

You wear a smile as a mask to hide the pain, to hide the hurt

Like the stars in the sky hiding behind the clouds.

You laugh when you want to cry but you hide behind the mask of laughter.

It is a masquerade show.

The pain hidden behind a nervous laugh

You pretend with a laugh and a smile.

The smile on your face is only there to fool everyone around you.

It is a masquerade show

It is ok to cry, to cry it's ok.

Like a ground covered with autumn leaves, hidden, pain hide.

Like a sleeping volcano hiding behind the beautiful mountain, pain is hidden

Pain is not like sweets shared in a playground.

You cannot see pain it is invisible, but you can feel the aching of it.

You can numb the pain through various means like an injection after the removal of a tooth.

An epidural to numb the pain of giving birth.

Climbing into a drink bottle to numb your pain or

getting lost in the Bermuda triangle of drugs to get rid of your pain

But none of it has made a difference

It is ok to cry, to cry it's ok

You are numb from the pain, but you hide it well.

The pain that you have hidden for so long has become normal for you.

The pain that you do not want anyone to see, you do not want anyone to know.

Pain have you hiding behind the door of anger.

Angry at everyone and everything.

Pain! angry! hiding!

Hiding! pain! angry!

It is ok to cry, to cry it's ok

You are shut in by pain.

Pain has you hiding in a corner of your room, curtains closed, loves ones and friends an enemy.

Phone ringing no reply, no answer from your front door, pain have you in isolation.

Locked in with your emotions, its, keeping you a prisoner, but you are the jailer holding the key, pain hides.

It is ok to cry, to cry it's ok.

Behind your dark cloud, the sun is coming out

And the rainbow of change will be across your sky.

INVOLVE

Involve, it could either be a good thing or like a bag filled with regrets, regrets, regrets.

If I did not get involved with you, I would have gone to university.

If I did not get involved with you, we would not be married.

If I did not get involved with you and the other gang members, my home would not have been the prison.

If I did not get involved with you, I would have finished my studies.

 If I did not get involved with you, I would have had my own business.

If I did not get involved with you, I would have had money.

If I did not get involved with you, I would have got further in life than I am now.

I got involved with you and lost myself.

I did not listen when they told me not to get involved with you.

And now I am saying, if only I had listened.

WHO ARE YOU TO YOU?

You look in the mirror and you do not see you.

You are invisible to you.

You are your mother's daughter.

You are your mother's son.

You are your brother's brother.

You are your sister's sister.

You are your daughters' mother.

You are your son's dad.

You are your grandson's grandmother.

You are your granddaughter's granddad.

Who are you, to you?

It is like there is a mist in front of you like a wall hiding you.

You are standing there but who are you.

You look at yourself in the mirror, you only see a reflection of you.

But who are you to you?

Evil hides on the inside and bold enough to live on the outside in many different forms, like a chameleon."

DOMESTIC ABUSE

DOMESTIC ABUSE, VERBAL ABUSE, EMOTIONAL ABUSE, MENTAL ABUSE, PHYSICAL ABUSE

DOMESTIC ABUSE WHY?

Is it because you are very insecure?

Is it because your self-esteem is low?

Domestic abuse why?

Love changes into the appearance of: Control, Resentment, Jealously, Intimidation, Manipulation, The guilty trips.

Why would you want to hurt the one you say you loved?

Why would you want to see them sad, broken and living in fear?

Scars of life like a tattoo on the body, stays with the children.

Portrait of negative memories locked away.

Domestic abuse why?

Is it easier to blame others than look at yourself?

Is it easier to see the mistake of others and the wrong things they do and not see yours?

Domestic abuse why?

The door of your ears shut from hearing the crying.

The door of your eyes shut from seeing the pain.

The door of your heart shut from feelings of love once felt.

Domestic abuse why?

THE MORNING.

I look for you the morning; from the moment my feet gently touch the floor.

I look for you.

I watch the night as it passes by.

I wait for you.

Waiting for the transition from night to day, as sleep

takes its cue from you and leave for a while before returning.

Hearing the chattering of birds and their singing of sweet melody.

I look for you, the morning.

THE LENSES OF MY EYES

The lenses of my eyes followed your movements.

You stopped for a moment, sitting there still, waiting, looking.

I wondered what you are thinking about then you suddenly up

and flew away.

The camera of my eyes followed you until you disappeared in the distance

Continuing along with the camera of my eyes, I silently let the lenses zoom in on what you were doing, like a camera crew the lenses followed you as you walked slowly back and forth. You stood still, staring, looking around unaware that the lenses of my eyes were fixed on you, capturing your every movement.

As I was wondering what you were thinking about, you turned around and slowly walked away looking, searching. I suppose you are fantasizing a buffet meal left on the side of the pavement, in the front garden, in the back garden waiting for you. The throw away of unwanted food.

HOW DID I GET HERE?

Some things that happened to you, you wonder and ask yourself the question. How did I get here? When did I get here? What am I doing here?

Were you sleepwalking and woke up on the edge of a mountain looking down, but you are afraid of heights? Sleepwalking and find yourself standing in a pool of water and you cannot swim. You are sleepwalking sitting in the driver's seat of a car and going 70 miles an hour, you stop.

"What am I doing here?"

You find yourself standing on the stage, all eyes on you, stage fright you cannot move and ask yourself this question.

"What am I doing here?"

You have been waiting awhile for the bus and when it comes you jump on without seeing the number of the bus, sit down and take out your newspaper, you are engrossed in what you are reading then glance up from the paper, nothing looked familiar, you looked around and noticed the number of the bus you were on was not your bus.

It is like realising after a few years in a relationship that you have been looking at too many soap dramas and in love with love, planning your wedding day, your wedding list and who would be invited to your wedding. The wedding venue, the wedding dress, the wedding cake, and the wedding speech in your mind, thinking Prince Charming had come at last to save you, sleeping beauty. Sleep walking and daydreaming at the same time, in a love daze. Your eyes were surely closed when you got involved in the relationship, now your eyes are opened, and you ask yourself.

"How did this happen? How did I get here?"

You bought the house because of the garden it was big! You did not notice the inside it did not cross your mind to look around the house thoroughly.

 The garden was big beautiful and clean it is what you have always wanted and it caught your attention. You fell in love at first sight, the garden did it for you and the house having a lot of space too.

Then you moved in and discovered that the house needed a lot of repairs and money to get it looking liveable. You had convinced yourself that the mortgage, would not be a problem but you were fooling yourself, you really could not afford it.

It all becomes too much to handle and you say to yourself.

"How, did this happen?"

 You thought you had checked everything out, you had a list of what to look out for but the distraction with the garden and the room sizes cause you to lose sight of what was important. You say to yourself,

"How, did this happen? How did I get here?"

You go to the job interview, the money sounds good, the perks, and the working time great. You would be leaving work early enough to meet up with friends and family, everything sounded like you landed yourself a dream job. With childish excitement, you go off and tell your friends and they celebrate with you.

Hoping to make them jealous you tell them how much you would be earning. And now you would be able to pay off your bills, go on holiday, buy a car. Then after a few months at the job, you find yourself being the last person to leave the office or place of work. The chance of meeting up with friends after work is not an option and non-existence. The heavy workload, increased bit by bit, then suddenly it got too much and earning a good salary now did not seem so great. It did not make up for lost time. The hoover had not seen the floor for a long time and you think you had forgotten how to use the washing machine your clothes piling up. Then you say to yourself,

"What am I doing here?

"How did I get here?

You go out and get yourself a credit card and exceed the limit of the card the interest is high. Worried, you get a second job but it seem to take longer to pay off the card so you borrow money from the bank of friends, bank of mum and bank of dad, even the bank of kids, with a promise to pay back you hope, saving you from falling into the river of debt. Tired; seems to be the only word that you know. Then you say to yourself,

"How did this happen?"

"How did I get here?"

Every time you go to cross the road, you would stand still, wait, listen, and look first before crossing. You would not step out and try and cross a busy road, for if you do, the consequences of your action could be fatal to yourself.

When you wait listen and look.

You would not find yourself saying

"What am I doing here? When did I get here? How did I get here? How did this happen?"

FORGOTTEN MEMORIES

The woman sat for a moment staring at the floor amused, this was a lovely surprise she thought to herself as she sat there. She switched on the DVD in her mind, she looked at different episodes of her life and found it. It happened to be tucked away in the storage part of her memory, put away in the archives of her life.

She had forgotten that it was there, the many years passed had covered it, like layers of dust in an untouched room. She smiled to herself then her heart started to race as if she was in panic and had difficulty breathing. She wondered to herself why this was! Why was she feeling this way? Then it suddenly hit her.

She remembered when she got the news, she was beside herself, it felt like a punch to her chest. This cannot be happening, it cannot be true, she was in shock, she was secretly hoping that it was a mistake or maybe she was dreaming, in a minute she would wake up.

A voice inside her shouted.

"Oh no!"

"This room is filled with too many people," she whispered to herself.

 She thought she would leave quietly, stop all communications she certainly did not like the script of the drama that was unveiling before her and was not going to stay around, to find out how it would end.

There is something about memory, it is like a film or favourite television programme you record because you enjoy it so much that you watch it again, again and again. Fond memories you recall and laugh to yourself, call a friend and reminisce about the good time, the funny times, the out of the ordinary things that happen to us, a surprise celebration, a surprise gift, a good deed done for you, you are happy to remember it.

Then there are those memories that make you sad every time you think about them, that you bury them blocking them out completely, you do not want to remember them.

Some memories you want them locked away like a double life sentence never to see daylight again.

Sharing sad or bad memories are not like sharing cake.

This memory, she did not share with anyone and had no intention of doing so.

ENCOURAGING WORDS FOR YOU:

"Remember you are brilliant."

"Laughing is good for you."

"To not try, is to fail."

"You are unique."

"There is only one you and you are priceless."

"Stop putting yourself down."

"Always appreciate the little things."

"When life seems upside down, take back control."

"Don't ever give up on you."

"Words of encouragement is better than words of discouragement."

www.ingramcontent.com/pod-product-compliance
Lightning Source LLC
Chambersburg PA
CBHW050020040726
47599CB00014B/1478